Faye,

Give thanks for a little
and you will find a lot!

Miranda Withers

Mom and Dad-

Thank you for teaching me the important things in life,

Like how to be a friend, a mother, and a wife!

Cathy and Rich-

You will always be "Mom and Dad" to me too,

Thank you for your love and everything you do!

WWW.MASCOTBOOKS.COM

PAWS and THINK!®: Be Thankful For What You Have

For more information, please contact:
Mascot Books
620 Herndon Parkway #320
Herndon, VA 20170
info@mascotbooks.com

CPSIA Code: PBANG0618A
Library of Congress Control Number: 2018903788
ISBN-13: 978-1-68401-921-2

Printed in the United States

PAWS and THINK!

BE THANKFUL FOR WHAT YOU HAVE

MIRANDA MITTLEMAN

ILLUSTRATED BY INDOS STUDIOS

Sometimes there are places
that are simply too far,

So I gather my family
and we hop in the car.

One of the best spots we go
is the local pet store.

There are beds and treats
and toys and more!

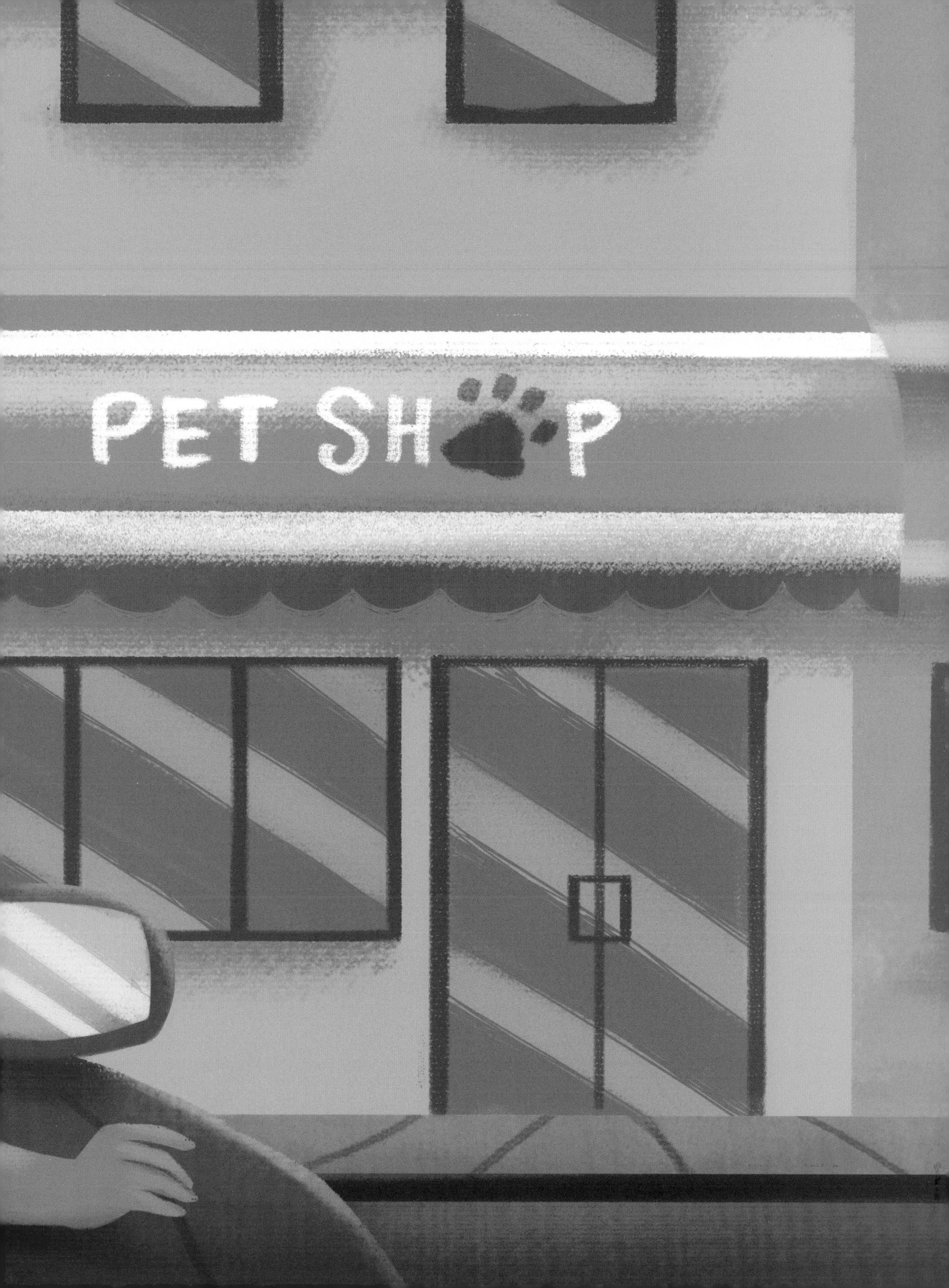
PET SH P

The friendly store owner is nice and quick,

Always ready to trade a treat for a trick!

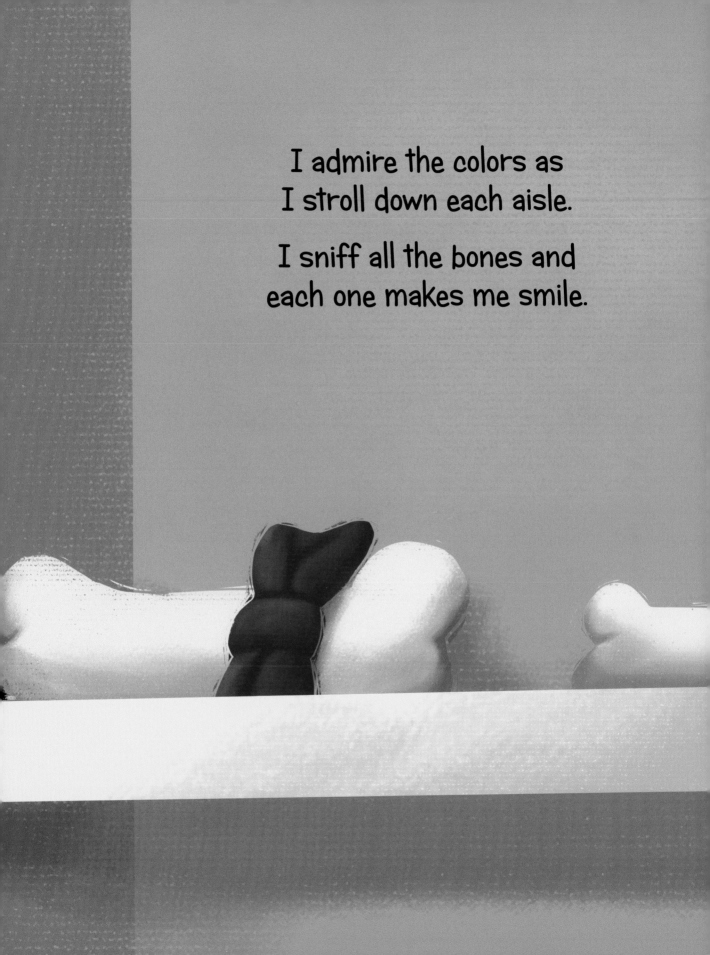

I admire the colors as
I stroll down each aisle.

I sniff all the bones and
each one makes me smile.

Somehow I always end up at the toys

And pick out a new one that makes lots of noise!

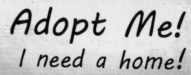

This time as we left,
I saw a puppy sitting alone

With a sign on the crate that said
"Adopt me! I need a home!"

He had no family and I could
tell that he was sad.

No brothers, no sisters,
not even a mom or a dad.

I barked, "It'll be okay!"
and gave him my new toy to chew.

Then I said, "I met a great family
and so will you!"

Adopt Me!
I need a home!

I have a place to call home
and a loving family,

And I'm so happy for
everything they have given me!

So the next time you find yourself
wanting something more,

PAWS and THINK! You already
have lots to be thankful for!

Miranda Mittleman grew up in Baltimore, Maryland, where she earned her bachelor's degree in marketing from Towson University. She's an avid runner, has a black belt in karate, and was even a contestant on *Wheel of Fortune!* But her true passion has always been poetry. She can recite most poems from her childhood by heart and was inspired to write the ***PAWS and THINK!***® series while living in the city with her husband, Michael, and their playful mutt, Weaver.

Check out Weaver's other adventures!

See what lesson I dig up next!